Favorite Stories from
Cowgirl Kate
and Cocoa
Spring Babies

Favorite Stories from Cowgirl Kate and Cocoa

Spring Babies

IOWA CITY

JUL -- 2016

PUBLIC LIBRARY

Written by **Erica Silverman**

Painted by **Betsy Lewin**

Green Light Readers
Houghton Mifflin Harcourt
Boston   New York

First Green Light Readers Edition, 2016

www.hmhco.com

The text type was set in Filosofia Regular.
The illustrations in this book were done in watercolors
on Strathmore one-ply Bristol paper.

The Library of Congress cataloged the hardcover edition of *Cowgirl Kate and Cocoa: Spring Babies* as follows:
Silverman, Erica.
Cowgirl Kate and Cocoa: spring babies/Erica Silverman: painted by Betsy Lewin.
p. cm.
ISBN: 978-0-15-205396-3 hardcover
ISBN: 978-0-547-56685-6 paperback
Summary: Cowgirl Kate and her horse Cocoa watch over the new calves, a puppy, and some baby barn owls. [1. Animals—Infancy—Fiction. 2. Cowgirls—Fiction. 3. Horses—Fiction.] I. Lewin, Betsy, ill. II. Title.
PZ7.S58625Cot2010
[E]—dc22
2009008399

ISBN: 978-0-544-66845-4 GLR paper over board
ISBN: 978-0-544-66844-7 GLR paperback

Manufactured in China
SCP 10 9 8 7 6 5 4 3 2 1

4500575156

To Allyn, Andrea, Sam, Betsy—

the best ranch crew ever! —E.S.

To Patty and Erica again, and to Dilys Evans.

It was a great ride. —B.L.

No More Calves!

"Cocoa, wake up," said Cowgirl Kate.

"We're going on night watch."

Cocoa opened his eyes.

He yawned.

"It's the middle of the night," he said.

"The cows should be sleeping."

"Tell that to the cows," said Cowgirl Kate.

"I would," said Cocoa, "but I don't want
to wake them up."

Cowgirl Kate put on Cocoa's saddle.
She led him outside.
"Cows sometimes have their calves at night,"
she said.

"No more calves!" cried Cocoa.

"They are too much work."

"Tell that to the cows," said Cowgirl Kate.

"I would," said Cocoa.

"But *that* would be too much work!"

Cowgirl Kate rode Cocoa to the spring pasture.

Mooo!

"That sounds like Sweety Pie," said Cocoa.

Moooooo!

"We have to find her!" said Cowgirl Kate.

Cowgirl Kate and Cocoa followed the sound of the mooing . . .

down a gully . . .

behind a bush.

"Sweety Pie!" cried Cowgirl Kate.

Sweety Pie walked around in circles.

She lay down.

She stood up.

She lay down again.

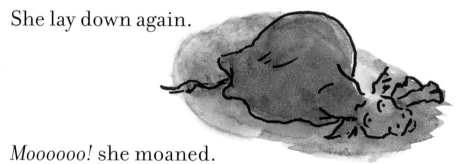

Moooooo! she moaned.

"Uh-oh!" cried Cocoa.

"I see a little calf head.

 I see little calf hooves."

 Cowgirl Kate grabbed her walkie-talkie.

"Mom! Dad!" she called.

"Come to the spring pasture!

 Sweety Pie has started to calve!"

 Cowgirl Kate slipped out of the saddle.

"Hold on, Sweety Pie," she said.

"Mom and Dad will be here soon."

"Too late!" said Cocoa.

"Look!"

A small wet calf was lying on the ground.
Sweety Pie licked him all over.
The calf opened his eyes.

He gazed at Sweety Pie.
He gazed at Cocoa.
He bobbed his head up and down.
Cocoa nickered.
"That little one needs us," he said.
"Let's stay and watch him until morning."

Cowgirl Kate smiled.

"Didn't you say calves are too much work?"
she asked.

"They *are* too much work," said Cocoa.

"And they are also sweet."

He leaned closer to Cowgirl Kate.

"But . . ." he whispered,

"I will *never* tell that to the cows!"

Ghost!

One night, Cocoa galloped out of the barn.
"Ghost!" he cried. "Ghost!"
Peppermint scrambled out after him.
"Arf!" she barked. "Arf!"

Cowgirl Kate came out of the house.

"Cocoa, what happened?" she asked.

"First I heard a spooky *hssssss,*" said Cocoa.

"Arf!" barked Peppermint.

"And then a ghost floated over my head."

"Arf!" barked Peppermint.

"Let me see this ghost," said Cowgirl Kate.

She went into the barn and turned on the light.

Cocoa stood in the doorway.

He peered inside.

Peppermint hid behind Cocoa.

"Don't be scared," said Cowgirl Kate.

Cocoa snorted.

"I am not scared!" he said.

Hssssss.

"That's the ghost!" cried Cocoa.

"Arf!" barked Peppermint.

"That sound came from the loft,"
said Cowgirl Kate.

She climbed up the ladder.

"Oh, my!" she whispered.

"One, two, three, four, five," she counted.

"Five ghosts?" cried Cocoa.

"Five babies," said Cowgirl Kate.

"Five baby ghosts?" cried Cocoa.

"No," said Cowgirl Kate.

"Come see."

Cocoa put his front hooves on a bale of hay
and stretched out his neck.

"Those are not ghosts," he said.

"They're barn owls," whispered Cowgirl Kate.

"But what about the ghost that floated over
my head?" asked Cocoa.
"That was their mama," said Cowgirl Kate.
"She flew outside to find food for her babies."

Hssssss, hissed the baby owls. *Hssssss*.

"What do they want?" asked Cocoa.

"They want their mama," said Cowgirl Kate.

Cocoa gazed at them.

"Your mama will come back," he said.
"But while she is out,
 I will watch you."
"Arf!" barked Peppermint.
"Peppermint will watch you, too," said Cocoa.

"We will *all* be on night watch,"
said Cowgirl Kate.
"I love night watch," said Cocoa.
"And I love spring babies!"

Erica Silverman is the author of a series of books about Cowgirl Kate and Cocoa, the original of which received a Theodor Seuss Geisel Honor. She is also the author of *Lana's World: Let's Go Fishing* and *Lana's World: Let's Have a Parade*, the first two titles in a delightful new easy reader series from Green Light Readers.
Erica's numerous picture books include the Halloween favorite *Big Pumpkin*. She lives in Los Angeles, California.

Betsy Lewin is the well-known illustrator of Doreen Cronin's *Duck for President*; *Giggle, Giggle, Quack*; and *Click, Clack, Moo: Cows That Type*, for which she received a Caldecott Honor. She lives in Brooklyn, New York.

More Green Light Readers by Erica Silverman!

More reading fun with great characters in favorite Level 2 series!

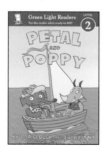 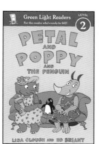  

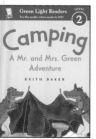 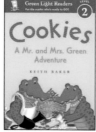